THE SHRINKING SUPERHERO

The brothers followed the crowd to the Green Crawler balloon. A crew was pumping it up with helium from a huge tank.

Frank and Joe watched, wide-eyed. It took lots of helium to fill those green muscles, but soon the boys' favorite superhero was rising off the ground.

"Whoa!" Frank exclaimed.

The Green Crawler hovered a few inches above the grass—until he began shriveling right before everyone's eyes!

"Frank," Joe gasped, "the Green Crawler is . . . shrinking!"

D0388631

CATCH UP ON ALL THE HARDY BOYS® SECRET FILES

#1 Trouble at the Arcade

#2 The Missing Mitt

#3 Mystery Map

#4 Hopping Mad

#5 A Monster of a Mystery

#6 The Bicycle Thief

#7 The Disappearing Dog

#8 Sports Sabotage

#9 The Great Coaster Caper

#10 A Rockin' Mystery

#11 Robot Rumble

#12 Lights, Camera . . . Zombies!

#13 Balloon Blow-Up

THE HARDY BOYS®

SECRET FILES #13

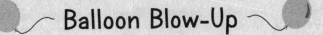

Balloon Blow-Up

BY FRANKLIN W. DIXON

ILLUSTRATED BY SCOTT BURROUGHS

ALADDIN • NEW YORK LONDON TORONTO SYDNEY NEW DELHI

If you purchased this book without a cover, you should be aware that this book is stolen property. It was reported as "unsold and destroyed" to the publisher, and neither the author nor the publisher has received any payment for this "stripped book."

This book is a work of fiction. Any references to historical events, real people, or real places are used fictitiously. Other names, characters, places, and events are products of the author's imagination, and any resemblance to actual events or places or persons, living or dead, is entirely coincidental.

🪔ALADDIN

An imprint of Simon & Schuster Children's Publishing Division
1230 Avenue of the Americas, New York, NY 10020
First Aladdin paperback edition December 2013
Text copyright © 2013 by Simon & Schuster, Inc.
Illustrations copyright © 2013 by Scott Burroughs
Series design by Lisa Vega
Cover design by Jeanine Henderson
All rights reserved, including the right of reproduction in whole or in part in any form.
ALADDIN is a trademark of Simon & Schuster, Inc., and related logo is a registered trademark of Simon & Schuster, Inc.
THE HARDY BOYS is a registered trademark of Simon & Schuster, Inc.
For information about special discounts for bulk purchases, please contact Simon & Schuster Special Sales at 1-866-506-1949 or business@simonandschuster.com.
The Simon & Schuster Speakers Bureau can bring authors to your live event. For more information or to book an event contact the Simon & Schuster Speakers Bureau at 1-866-248-3049 or visit our website at www.simonspeakers.com.
The text of this book was set in Garamond.
Manufactured in the United States of America 1113 OFF
10 9 8 7 6 5 4 3 2 1
Library of Congress Control Number 2013939358
ISBN 978-1-4424-5371-5
ISBN 978-1-4424-5372-2 (eBook)

CONTENTS

1   MALL MADNESS   1

2   SUPERHERO, SUPERZERO!   10

3   GREEN CRAWLER FALLER   19

4   BLAMED AND FRAMED   31

5   CLAWS AND CLUES   39

6   UNDERCOVER BROTHERS   50

7   ZOOM AND GLOOM   63

8   MUSICAL SCARES   70

9   BURIED TREASURE   78

10   RAID ON PARADE   88

1

Mall Madness

Check it out, you guys!" nine-year-old Frank Hardy said. "Soon we're going to meet the Crawler in the flesh!"

"*Green* flesh!" Frank's eight-year-old brother, Joe, said with a grin.

It was Saturday morning. Frank and Joe were at the Bayport Mall. The boys' friends Chet and Iola Morton were also there, along with about a hundred other kids.

They weren't at the mall to see the new electronic

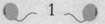

games or sneaker styles. They were there to meet the most awesome superhero, the Green Crawler!

"Do you think the Crawler will do what he does in the movies?" Chet asked, digging into a bag of Cheesy Curls.

"You mean grow extra legs five times the normal size?" Iola asked. "And climb walls and ceilings faster than a spider?"

"Sure," Frank said. "As long as Mo Mantis doesn't try to stop him."

Chet let out a "Boo!" Mo Mantis was the Green Crawler's biggest enemy. Mo was part human, part praying mantis, and his dream was to destroy the Green Crawler. Thanks to the Crawler, it was a dream that never came true.

"Remember," Iola said. "We're not here just to see the Crawler. We're here to find out who won the contest!"

"How could we forget?" Joe said. "We all drew

a picture of the Green Crawler. And the kid with the best picture wins the big prize," he went on. "A chance to march with the Green Crawler balloon in the Fall Fest parade."

The Fall Fest parade happened every October in Bayport. It had floats and the high school marching band, plus one supersize balloon.

"I've always wanted to be one of those balloon handlers," Chet said, and sighed. He crossed his cheesy fingers. "I hope I win."

"Me too," Joe said. He pulled something from his back pocket. It looked like a green claw on a stick. "That's why I brought this."

"What is it?" Iola asked, wrinkling her nose.

"It's my Green Crawler snapping claw!" Joe said, squeezing the handle to make it open and close. "The Green Crawler is the only one who can use Mo Mantis's own claw against him. It's also my lucky charm!"

"You don't need luck to win this contest, Joe," Frank said. "Just the best drawing of the Green Crawler."

Joe pictured himself as a balloon handler. Neat! But then he had a scary thought . . .

"What if the balloon picks me up and carries me away?" Joe asked. "I'm just a kid!"

"The other handlers will all be grown-ups," Frank said with a chuckle. "That's what it said in the rules."

"Hopefully, big and strong grown-ups," Chet said. "I heard the Green Crawler balloon is humongous!"

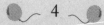

They were about to move closer to the stage when a bunch of voices began shouting: "We want Nutty! We want Nutty back in the parade!"

"Who are they?" Chet asked as some kids marched by holding signs. "And why are they wearing squirrel hats?"

"It's the Nutty the Squirrel fan club," Frank explained.

"You mean that cartoon squirrel?" Iola asked. "The Nutty the Squirrel balloon was in the parade two years in a row."

"That's why the fan club is here, I guess," Frank decided. "They want the Nutty balloon back in the parade."

"They can dream on," Chet declared. "The Green Crawler wipes the floor with that Nutty the Squirrel!"

"Shh!" Iola warned. "They might hear you!"

Too late. The fans stopped shouting. A boy

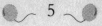

wearing glasses and the biggest squirrel hat glared at Chet as he walked over.

"Here comes Sammy Kernkraut," Joe murmured. "He's the president of the Nutty club."

"How do you know?" Frank asked.

"He's in my class," Joe said. "He carries a Nutty lunchbox and wears a different Nutty T-shirt every day."

Sammy stopped in front of Chet. He planted his hands on his hips, then said, "Oh yeah? Nutty the Squirrel can stuff a hundred acorns into his mouth—and whistle the Nutty theme song at the same time."

"Oh yeah?" Chet shot back. "The Green Crawler can climb a skyscraper in thirty seconds!"

"Nutty can do it in ten seconds!" Sammy snapped.

As Chet and Sammy continued to argue, Joe

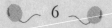

turned to Frank. "Too bad there can't be two balloons in the parade," he whispered.

"Oof!" Frank grunted as someone bumped past him. He frowned when he saw Adam Ackerman—the biggest bully at Bayport Elementary School. With him was his friend, the second-biggest bully, Tony Riccio.

Adam and Tony pushed their way through the crowd toward the stage, stepping on several toes along the way.

"Why don't you look where you're going?" Frank yelled.

"Why don't you mind your own business," Adam shot back, "detectives Hardy and Hardy?"

Frank rolled his eyes. Adam was always teasing him and Joe about solving mysteries. Probably because he was always the suspect.

"What if Adam wins and gets to be a balloon

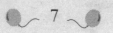

handler?" Frank asked, and frowned.

"Adam?" Joe snorted. "He's got enough hot air to be his own balloon!"

Sammy walked by, holding Chet's bag of Cheesy Curls. Chet was holding a small bag of Nutty Squirrel Nuts.

"What happened?" Frank asked.

"We made a truce," Chet said, popping a nut into his mouth. "But Sammy still wants Nutty in the parade."

A tune suddenly blared from the loudspeaker. It was the Green Crawler theme song.

"We want the Green Crawler!" Joe yelled. Soon all the kids, except those in the Nutty the Squirrel fan club, were cheering for the Crawler too!

The cheering grew louder as a trapdoor in the stage floor slowly opened.

"Here he comes!" Joe shouted.

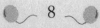

A thick gray mist covered the stage. Through it the outline of a figure could be seen.

"It's him!" Chet said. "It's the Crawler!"

Joe looked harder, then shook his head.

"That's not the Green Crawler," Joe said. "That's the villain—Mo Mantis!"

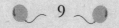

2

Superhero, Superzero!

Booooo!" the kids shouted as Mo stepped forward.

"Greetings, Bayport!" Mo laughed, waving his steely sharp claws at the crowd. "Eeeeeevil greetings!"

Joe stared at Mo. With his mantis mask and hood, he looked exactly like he did in the Green Crawler movies!

"Boo and hiss all you want!" Mo declared. He

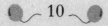

pressed his pointy hands together. "I'm praaaaaay-ing that the Green Crawler balloon is destroyed so I can fly over Bayport in all my villainous glory!"

Suddenly—*poof!* A thick cloud of green smoke swallowed up Mo Mantis.

"Where did he go?" Frank wondered out loud.

The smoke cleared. Mo was gone. In his place was—

"The Green Crawler!" Joe exclaimed.

Everyone cheered as the Green Crawler stepped out of the smoke. Tucked in his enormous muscled arm was a giant can marked PEST SPRAY.

"You all know I'm one strong dude," the Green Crawler told the crowd. "Well, I'm looking for a strong kid to hold down my balloon in the Fall Fest parade!"

Hands shot up as kids shouted, "Me! Me! Me!"

"Then what are we waiting for?" the Green

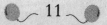

Crawler said. "Let this mean green contest begin!"

Another man joined the Green Crawler. He was introduced as Mitch Snyder, the owner of Snyder's Department Store. The biggest department store in Bayport sponsored the Fall Fest parade every year.

"Hey, kids," Mitch said, holding up a big envelope. "I've got the winning drawing right here."

Joe wished he had X-ray vision. Was the winning drawing his?

"Everyone take out your tickets," Mitch went on. "The ones with the numbers printed on them."

Frank was already holding his ticket, number sixty-five. "Why don't you take out your ticket?" he asked Joe.

"I don't have to," Joe said. "I know it's number sixty-six."

A hush fell over the crowd as Mitch opened the envelope. He looked inside, then said into the mike, "The winning drawing is . . . number sixty-six."

"Huh?" Joe said. Had he heard what he thought he'd just heard? His eyes lit up as Mitch pulled a drawing from the envelope. It was his drawing!

"Way to go, Joe!" Frank said, patting Joe's back. "Where's your ticket?"

Joe dug through his pockets. Where had he put his ticket?

"Um . . . I don't know." Joe gulped.

"What do you mean, you don't know?" Frank cried. "You need the number to win!"

Joe was about to panic when he remembered the pocket on the knee of his cargo pants. He reached in and—

"Here it is!" Joe sighed with relief. He tossed his lucky claw to Frank and squeezed through the crowd to the stage.

"And we have our winner!" the Crawler said after matching Joe's ticket to the numbered drawing. "What's your name, big guy?"

"Joe Hardy!" Joe said into the mike.

"Well, Joe," the Green Crawler said, "who will you pick to march with you in the parade? You get to choose one friend or relative."

"That would be my brother, Frank," Joe said.

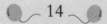

"We're not just brothers, we're detectives."

Frank smiled from the crowd. He and Joe made an awesome detective team—even though they were totally different. Frank was the serious, cautious type. Joe was serious too—about jumping into any mystery head-on!

"Detectives, huh?" The Green Crawler chuckled. "Maybe you can help me battle Mo Mantis one of these days!"

"Deal!" Joe said.

"Here you go, Joe," Mitch said, handing Joe a big brown envelope. "This will tell you all about the parade."

"Like what?" Joe asked excitedly.

"Like that there'll be a parade orientation next Saturday morning in the park at seven thirty," Mitch said. "We'll be blowing up the Green Crawler balloon for you to practice with."

"Thanks!" Joe said. He took the brown envelope

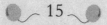

and then ran offstage to meet Frank.

"I guess this thing was lucky!" Frank said, tossing the Crawler claw back to Joe.

Joe grinned as he stuck his claw into his back pocket. He was about to look for Chet and Iola when he saw someone else. . . .

"Isn't that Mo Mantis over there?" Joe asked.

Frank followed Joe's gaze. Sure enough, leaning against the wall was Mo, sipping from a cup through his mask. The hand holding the cup was free of its glove.

"Cool," Frank said. "Let's go over and say hi."

The brothers hurried over to Mo.

"Hey, Mo," Joe said. "I'll bet you're drinking a sinister brew that'll make you eviler with each sip!"

Frank and Joe waited for Mo's reply. Instead, he silently glared at Joe through his mantis mask. Gulp.

"Let's go," Frank whispered.

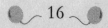

"Whoa," Joe said as they walked away. "Did you see those scary eyes?"

"And did you see the tattoo on his hand?" Frank asked.

"A tattoo?" Joe said. "Of what?"

"A praying mantis," Frank replied. "What else?"

Chet and Iola pushed through the crowd to get to Frank and Joe.

"I can't believe you won, Joe!" Iola said.

"Believe it, because here it is," Joe said as he held up the brown envelope. "The grand prize!"

Suddenly—

"Hey!" Joe cried as someone snatched the envelope out of his hand. Spinning around, Joe saw Adam and Tony. Adam was holding the brown envelope and grinning nastily.

"Give it back!" Joe demanded.

"No way!" Adam sneered. "I had the winning number!"

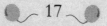

"You did not!" Joe said. "I had number sixty-six."

Adam shook his head. He used his free hand to hold up his ticket. "See? . . . Number sixty-six."

"That's number ninety-nine upside down," Iola snapped. "Nice try, Ackerman."

Joe tried to take the envelope, but Adam held it back.

"Come on, Adam!" Frank said angrily. "That was Joe's drawing of the Green Crawler they picked, not yours."

"You probably drew Mo Mantis, Adam," Chet said. "It takes a villain to know one."

Adam glared at Chet. He then raced off with the envelope, Tony right behind him.

Joe froze as he watched the bullies get away. That envelope had everything he needed to be in the parade!

"What are we waiting for, Joe?" Frank cried. "Let's get Adam—and that envelope!"

3

Green Crawler Faller

The Hardys and the Mortons chased the bullies through the mall. They darted past the sports store and the music shop, and even zigzagged through the tables in the food court.

"Stop!" Joe yelled.

Frank and Joe picked up speed. They were about to catch up with Adam and Tony when the two slipped inside an elevator.

"Rats!" Frank said as the doors began to close.

"Game over!" Adam laughed as he waved the envelope.

"Not yet!" Joe said. He thrust his Crawler claw between the closing doors. Adam gasped as the claw snatched the envelope from his hand!

"Hey!" Adam yelled as the doors closed.

Joe turned to Frank and his friends. He waved his trusty gadget with the envelope.

"I told you it was lucky!" Joe said.

The next Saturday morning couldn't come quickly enough for Joe and Frank. They could hardly sit still in the backseat of their dad's car as he drove them to parade practice.

"Do you have the envelope?" Fenton Hardy asked. "And your IDs?"

"Check!" Joe said, holding up the envelope.

"Check!" Frank said, lifting the ID around his neck.

"Your mom and I signed the permission slips," Mr. Hardy said as he drove. "Now, remember the parade organization's agreement that you both signed."

Frank nodded. "Any disrespectful behavior like vandalizing parade property means we're out of the parade," he said.

"Who do they think we are?" Joe joked. "Adam and Tony?"

Mr. Hardy dropped Frank and Joe off at the park. After saying good-bye, the brothers made their way toward the special parade tent. On the way the boys spotted a shiny red motorbike parked against a tree.

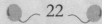

"Somebody rode here in style," Frank said.

But Joe had his eye on something else. It was big and green, and stretched out over a nearby field.

"Look, Frank!" Joe said. "That must be the Green Crawler balloon before it's blown up."

Some workers spread out the balloon, while others tethered it to the ground. Joe wondered if they were balloon handlers—just like him and Frank.

Also in the park were the parade floats. One was decorated to look like a pirate ship. Another had a castle with a big purple dragon on top.

The biggest float carried a small red barn and a haystack. Teenagers and kids dressed up like scarecrows practiced a dance while a girl with long brown hair sang.

"That's Taylor Smyth!" Frank said. "She's a huge star."

Joe shook his head as he pointed to the Crawler

balloon. "*That's* the biggest star in the parade," he said.

Frank and Joe were watching some clowns practicing handstands when they spotted Sammy and his Nutty the Squirrel fan club. The club members were walking quietly through the park, toward the balloon.

"What are they doing here?" Joe wondered.

The club stopped to stare at the Green Crawler balloon. After a signal from Sammy the kids turned and continued walking.

"Did you see them staring at that balloon?" Frank asked. "I hope they're not here to make trouble."

"Those kids?" Joe scoffed. "They make Nutty the Squirrel seem ferocious!"

Frank's eyes lit up as if he'd just remembered something. He pulled a camera out of his pocket. "I brought this to take pictures of the balloon."

"And I brought this," Joe said, pulling the Green Crawler claw from his back pocket. "My lucky charm."

"But you already won the contest!" Frank said.

Joe shrugged and said, "You can never be too lucky!"

The brothers entered a tent set up for parade volunteers. There to greet them was the parade director, Kevin Lively.

"Hi, guys," Kevin said. "Welcome to—"

"Excuse me, Mr. Lively!" a woman interrupted. She wore a blue-and-gold marching band uniform and a big scowl.

"Boys," Kevin said, "meet Kit Abernathy, the high school band director."

Kit nodded at Frank and Joe. She then turned to Kevin and said, "What's this about my band being followed by the Green Crawler balloon?"

"What's wrong with that?" Kevin asked.

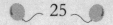

25

"All eyes will be on the balloon, not on the Bayport Boomerangs!" Kit complained while waving her conductor's baton in Kevin's face.

Joe gulped. That thing would make a dangerous weapon!

"My kids are musicians," Kit went on. "Not escorts for some giant green blob with legs!"

"Sorry, Kit," Kevin said. "But I can't change the lineup now."

"What?" Kit cried.

"One more thing," Kevin added. "Teach your band the Green Crawler theme song. It'll be perfect for the parade."

Kit angrily turned on her boot heel and huffed off.

"Not a Green Crawler fan," Kevin joked. He then introduced the brothers to someone much friendlier—Lynn Braun, the captain of the balloon handlers.

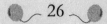

"How do handlers keep such huge balloons from flying away?" Frank asked.

"By getting a good grip," Lynn said, "and pulling down hard on the ropes attached to the balloon."

Joe flexed his arm. "We're just the guys for the job!" he declared.

"We'll go over the directions later," Lynn said, chuckling. "But here's Brett with your handler uniforms."

The guy named Brett carried two shopping bags over. One was marked JOE HARDY, the other FRANK HARDY.

The brothers looked inside their bags. Each had a green jumpsuit, thick work gloves, and a Green Crawler mask!

"The masks are cool," Joe said. "But how will anyone know it's us under them?"

"Easy," Brett said, and smirked. "You'll be the only little squirts handling the balloon."

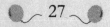 27

"Who are you calling squirts?" Joe complained.

"Kidding!" Brett said.

Joe could tell by Brett's eyes that he hadn't been kidding.

"May I take a picture of the Green Crawler balloon before it's blown up?" Frank asked Lynn.

"It's eight thirty," Lynn said with a glance at her watch. "You have an hour until we blow up the balloon."

"Cool!" Joe said. They were about to get up close and personal with the Green Crawler balloon!

"Just don't touch the balloon or step on it," Lynn added sternly.

The brothers left their bags inside the tent. On the way to the balloon, Frank took a picture of the Bayport Boomerangs practicing a song. But where was Kit?

"Take a picture of me in front of the balloon, Frank!" Joe called, already running toward it.

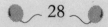

But as the brothers approached the balloon, they saw a big lump moving around underneath the material.

"What's that?" Frank asked.

The weird lump started moving to the other side of the balloon. Then suddenly out from under crawled Kit!

Kit glanced around quickly before standing up and hurrying away.

"What was Kit doing under there?" Frank wondered.

"Who knows?" Joe shrugged. "Come on, Frank. I'm ready for my close-up!"

"Okay," Frank said. "But remember what Lynn said. Don't step on the balloon!"

Joe was careful to stand inches away from the balloon. He pulled out his lucky claw and held it in the air. "Make sure you get this in the picture," he said.

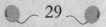

Frank was about to take the shot when—

"Say 'cheesy,' loser!" someone jeered.

Joe gasped as a pitchfork-wielding scarecrow leaped in front of him. The scarecrow jabbed his fork in Joe's direction, making Joe stumble back.

"Whoooaaaa!" Joe cried.

His lucky claw flew out of his hand as he felt himself falling—back onto the balloon!

4

Blamed and Framed

Great," Joe muttered as he lay flat on the thick nylon material.

"Joe, are you okay?" Frank called.

"I'm okay," Joe said, sitting up. "But is the balloon okay?"

Before checking the balloon, Joe glared at the scarecrow. He wore a floppy straw hat that covered most of his face. But when he laughed, Joe knew who he was.

"Adam!" Joe snapped.

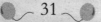 31

"Ba-ha-ha-ha-ha!" Adam laughed, swinging his pitchfork. "Hope you had a nice trip, Hardy!"

Frank took a step toward Adam, but the bully was already running away.

Joe stood up. He bent down to pick up his Crawler claw. That's when a voice shouted, "I told you not to touch that balloon!"

Looking up, Joe saw Lynn running over, followed by Kevin and Brett.

"It was an accident," Joe told them. "Someone scared me and I tripped."

Brett pointed to Joe's Crawler claw on the balloon. "That toy of his probably ripped the balloon," he accused.

"No, it didn't," Joe said, lifting the Crawler claw. "I don't see any rips anywhere."

"The balloon is made of thick nylon," Lynn told Kevin. "I doubt the toy ripped it."

"We'll find out," Brett said, "when we blow up the balloon."

Kevin waved to Joe. "Just get off the balloon carefully," he said.

Joe was careful as he stepped off. Kevin, Lynn, and Brett were already heading back to the tent.

"It's a good thing you didn't rip the balloon," Frank said. "Or we'd be out of the parade."

"Thanks to Adam," Joe said. "What was he doing here dressed as a goofy scarecrow?"

"The Taylor Smyth float," Frank reminded him. "Adam probably volunteered to be on it."

"Yeah, so he could make trouble." Joe frowned.

The last thing Frank and Joe wanted was more trouble. Instead of looking for Adam, they headed to the snack table. There they spoke to more volunteers, including clowns, float drivers, and two other scarecrows.

Frank decided he would ask the scarecrows about Adam, but just then someone shouted, "Hey, everybody! They're pumping up the balloon!"

"All right!" Joe cheered.

The brothers followed the crowd to the Green Crawler balloon. A crew was pumping it up with helium from a huge tank.

Frank and Joe watched, wide-eyed. It took lots of helium to fill those green muscles, but soon the boys' favorite superhero was rising off the ground.

"Whoa!" Frank exclaimed.

The Green Crawler hovered a few inches above the grass—until he began shriveling right before everyone's eyes!

"Frank," Joe gasped, "the Green Crawler is . . . shrinking!"

Fsssssss! Everyone's jaws dropped as the Green Crawler collapsed to the ground with a hiss.

"The balloon *was* punctured!" Lynn exclaimed.

Brett pointed a finger at Joe. "Thanks to that kid!" he growled.

"What?" Joe cried.

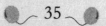

"He told you," Frank said to Brett. "It wasn't ripped."

"Will the other volunteers go back to their floats, please?" Kevin called out. "Will the Bayport Boomerangs clear the area too?"

"Come on, kids," Kit told the band. She smirked at the deflated balloon. "Maybe we won't have to learn that Green Crawler tune after all."

Frank and Joe waited until the others had left.

"Maybe the balloon was ripped in the factory," Joe told Lynn. "You said yourself it was made of thick nylon, so it would be hard for someone to rip it."

"The balloon was checked for rips in the factory," Lynn said. "And our handlers were very careful with it when they spread it out."

Kevin heaved a sigh. "We saw you messing around on that balloon, Joe," he said.

"But—" Joe started to say.

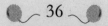

"I know you won the contest, Joe," Lynn cut in, "but you and your brother did sign an agreement."

"The one about disrespectful behavior?" Joe asked. He felt his heart sink. "Does this mean we're out of the parade?"

"I'm afraid so," Kevin said with a frown.

"Oh no!" Frank groaned.

Joe opened his mouth to speak. He was so upset, nothing came out.

"Excuse me," Frank said. "If Joe and I find the real person who ripped the balloon, can we march in the parade?"

"The real person?" Lynn repeated.

"We're detectives," Frank explained.

"Good ones!" Joe added.

"Sure, sure," Kevin said dismissively. "Go play detective."

Frank and Joe both frowned. *Play?*

"Can the rip be patched in time for the parade?" Kevin asked Lynn.

"Probably," Lynn said. "But since the parade is tomorrow, we'll have to work fast."

Frank turned to Joe and whispered, "So will we!"

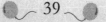

5

Claws and Clues

Frank and Joe turned in their IDs and handler uniforms—but they refused to lose hope.

"At least we still have a chance of being in the parade," Frank said as he and Joe made their way out of the park.

"First we have to find the real balloon slasher," Joe said. "Where do we start?"

"Where we always start," Frank said. "The six *W*s—Who, What, When, Where, Why, and How."

The six *W*s system was actually five *W*s and one *H*, but it was a lot easier to call it the six *W*s.

The system had been taught to Frank and Joe by their dad. Mr. Hardy was a private detective and sometimes helped the brothers with their cases. He had also helped build them a secret tree house in the woods behind the house. The tree house had become the brothers' detective headquarters. It was where they wrote the six *W*s on a big dry-erase board.

"I don't want to wait until we're in our tree house," Joe said impatiently. "I want to write the six *W*s now."

"But we didn't bring any pens or paper," Frank said as they passed the basketball court.

"Hmm," Joe said, looking around. That's when he saw a girl drawing on the basketball court with colored chalk.

"Joe, wait up!" Frank called as Joe began running toward the girl.

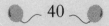

The girl was putting the finishing touches on a butterfly she was drawing as Frank and Joe hurried over.

"Excuse me," Joe said. "Can we borrow a piece of chalk?"

The girl pointed to the Green Crawler claw in Joe's pocket. "Sure," she said. "If you let me play with *that*!"

"Okay," Joe said. "Just be careful with it!" He exchanged the claw for a piece of green chalk. Green for the Green Crawler.

"Let's get to work," Frank declared.

They kneeled on the court, where Joe wrote the word "What."

"*What* happened?" Joe asked.

"Someone slashed the Green Crawler balloon when no one was looking," Frank decided.

Joe wrote that out. The next *W* was *When*. That was usually the toughest!

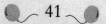 41

"We got to the park at seven thirty," Joe remembered. "The handlers were starting to spread out the balloon."

"It could have happened after they left the balloon," Frank suggested. "There was no one there when we went to take the picture."

"That was eight thirty," Joe said. "I remember Lynn telling us the time."

"Seven thirty . . . eight thirty," Frank thought out loud. "That means the balloon could have been slashed between—"

"Seven thirty and eight thirty," Joe cut in excitedly.

Joe's fingers turned green as he scribbled the time line on the court.

He then turned to Frank and said, "Next *W*— *Where* did it happen?"

"Lynn said the balloon was in good shape at

the factory," Frank said. "So the damage probably happened in the park."

Then Joe asked, "*Why* would anyone want to slash the Green Crawler balloon? And *How* did they slash it?"

"Maybe somebody wanted to get even with the parade," Frank said, and shrugged. "Kit was mad at Kevin for making the band march in front of the Green Crawler balloon."

"She also had that pointy baton," Joe said. "Pointy enough to poke a hole in the balloon."

"We saw her crawling underneath the balloon too," Frank pointed out. "Pretty suspicious, if you ask me."

Joe wrote Kit's name on the cement. He then looked up and said, "Maybe somebody didn't want to get even with the parade—but with us."

"Us?" Frank repeated.

"Adam was a sore loser when I won the contest," Joe said. "He was also carrying that sharp pitchfork."

"We know what a creep Adam can be too," Frank said. But as Joe wrote Adam's name, Frank thought of one more.

"What about Sammy and his Nutty the Squirrel fan club?" Frank asked. "They were here, checking out the Green Crawler balloon."

Joe began to write Sammy's name, and then said, "How do you spell 'Kernkraut?'"

"*K-e-r-n-k-r-a-u-t*!" a voice shouted.

"Huh?" Joe said. He turned to see the chalk girl walking over. She was smiling as she snapped Joe's Green Crawler claw.

"What are you, a spelling bee champ?" Joe asked.

"No, silly," the girl said. "Sammy Kernkraut is my brother. He's eight, and I'm five and three quarters."

"You're Sammy's sister?" Frank asked.

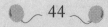

"Does that answer your question?" she asked. Using the claw, she pointed to her signature under the butterfly: Sadie Kernkraut.

Frank raised an eyebrow at Joe. Maybe Sadie could tell them what Sammy and the club had done.

"So, Sadie," Frank said. "What did your brother do this morning?"

"Sammy and the club usually watch the Nutty the Squirrel show every Saturday morning," Sadie said. She shook her head hard. "But not today."

"How come?" Joe asked.

"The club had something important to do," Sadie said. "Really, really important."

Joe urged her on. "What did they do?"

"Was it something with a giant balloon?" Frank asked.

"I'm not telling," Sadie said. She held up the Green Crawler claw. "Unless you give me this thing for keeps."

"Nuh-uh," Joe said, shaking his head. "No deal."

"Let her have it, Joe!" Frank urged.

"But it's my lucky charm!" Joe argued.

"How lucky could it be if you had it when we got fired?" Frank argued back. "And she might give us a great clue."

"Clue?" Sadie gasped. "Are you guys spies?"

Joe didn't answer. He just held out his hand and said, "Come on. Give it up."

"No claw, no clue," Sadie said. She gave Joe the claw, then pointed behind him. "Look. Here comes a scarecrow!"

Frank and Joe turned to see a kid dressed as a scarecrow walking in their direction. When they saw the pitchfork in his hand, they knew who it was!

"Adam Ackerman!" Frank declared.

When Adam saw the brothers, he narrowed his eyes. He then turned and ran the other way.

"He's not getting away this time!" Frank said.

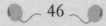

Joe dropped the chalk. In a flash he and Frank were chasing Adam through the park.

"Somebody stop that scarecrow!" Frank yelled as they charged past the playground.

Adam raced onto the parade practice field. So did Frank and Joe. Adam headed straight toward the Taylor Smyth hoedown float. So did Frank and Joe.

"We're catching up!" Frank said.

"Are we lucky or what?" Joe exclaimed.

Their luck ran out as a bunch of other scarecrows began dancing in their direction. Frank and Joe groaned as the scarecrows from the hoedown float blocked their way!

"Get out of the way—please!" Joe shouted.

"*You* get out of the way," one of the scarecrows shouted over the canned music. "We're practicing here!"

The brothers scurried around the scarecrows. But the scarecrow they wanted was gone.

"Maybe he's on the float," Joe said.

The brothers climbed up onto the hoedown float. They didn't see Adam, but they saw his pitchfork leaning against the barn.

"Careful," Joe said as Frank reached for the pitchfork. "That thing is sharp."

"No, it's not," Frank said as he flicked the prongs. "These things are made out of rubber!"

"Rubber?" Joe cried. He felt a prong to see for himself. It was soft and rubbery—and it bounced!

"Adam couldn't have ripped the balloon with this fork," Frank said, leaning the pitchfork back on the barn.

"I still don't trust Adam," Joe said. "Maybe he had a pair of scissors in his pocket or something else sharp."

"There's only one way to find out," Frank said. He pounded on the barn door and yelled, "Open up! Open up!"

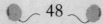

"Or we'll open it for you!" Joe shouted.

Frank and Joe pounded and shouted—until two tall shadows slowly loomed over them.

Turning, the brothers gulped. Behind them were two big guys wearing leather jackets and dark shades. The one chewing a toothpick gazed down at them and said through gritted teeth:

"Looking for someone, fellas?"

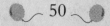

6

Undercover Brothers

Frank and Joe stared up at the guys.

"Um—we were looking for the person who ripped the Green Crawler balloon!" Joe blurted.

"We think he's hiding in the barn!" Frank said.

The barn door creaked open. Was Adam giving himself up? But instead of Adam stepping out, it was—

"Taylor Smyth!" Joe gasped.

Taylor wore a red-and-white plaid shirt, jean

shorts, and a big smile. "Hi, boys," she said. "I see you've met my bodyguards, Dash and Boris."

Joe heard a snicker. He turned to see Adam peeking out from behind the barn.

"There he is!" Joe said, pointing. "There's the guy who ripped the Green Crawler balloon!"

Adam coolly strolled out from behind the barn. "Who, me?" he asked innocently.

The other scarecrows had stopped dancing. They stood on the float, watching everything.

"Go ahead, Boris and Dash," Frank said. "Check Adam's pockets for scissors or something else sharp."

Another scarecrow let out a laugh.

"Good luck with that!" he said. "Our scarecrow costumes have no pockets!"

"Yeah!" a teenage scarecrow with a flowered hat complained. "I have nowhere to put my cell phone."

"Or my gum!" a younger scarecrow added.

"That was my idea, you guys," Taylor said, and smiled. "I don't want any snacking or texting on my float."

"Want to check my pockets now, losers?" Adam sneered at Frank and Joe.

"And no name-calling on my float, either," Taylor scolded Adam.

The bodyguards now loomed over Adam.

"What are you doing back here, anyway?" Boris demanded. "You were fired."

"Fired?" Joe asked.

"He tied my manager's shoelaces together earlier this morning," Taylor said. "What a pest!"

"I'm going, I'm going!" Adam groaned.

"Don't forget to return your costume at the tent." Dash pointed two fingers at his own eyes, then at Adam's. "I'll be watching you, wise guy!"

Adam stomped his way out of the barn.

"We'd better go too," Frank murmured to Joe.

"Wait!" Joe said. "We forgot something important."

"We did?" Frank asked. "What?"

"We forgot to get Taylor's autograph!" Joe said with a smile.

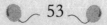

53

Taylor was happy to give Frank and Joe signed pictures. The brothers thanked Taylor, then left to meet their parents outside the park.

"How did parade practice go?" Fenton Hardy asked as the boys climbed into the backseat of the car.

Frank and Joe traded embarrassed looks.

"Well," Frank said slowly, "we got to meet Taylor Smyth."

"Taylor who?" Mrs. Hardy asked.

"She's a singer, Mom," Joe explained. He took a deep breath before adding, "Um . . . we also got fired from the parade."

"What?" Mr. and Mrs. Hardy exclaimed at the same time.

Frank explained all about Adam's causing Joe to fall on the balloon, and how everyone blamed Joe.

"I'm sure the balloon wasn't ripped after I fell on it," Joe said.

"Hmm," Fenton said as he drove. "Sounds like you guys were framed."

"Do you want your father and me to talk to Mr. Lively?" Mrs. Hardy asked over her shoulder.

"No thanks, Mom," Frank said. "We want to find the real balloon ripper ourselves."

"So the Hardy brothers are on the case." Fenton smiled. "Do you have any suspects?"

"Only two left, Dad," Joe said. "Kit the bandleader and the Nutty the Squirrel fan club."

"We'll never be able to question the club," Frank said. "Sammy Kernkraut knows we're not big Nutty fans."

"We can *pretend* we want to join the club," Joe said. "I've heard them talk about it and they meet every Saturday at Sammy's house at eleven."

"But we don't know where Sammy lives," Frank said.

"I do," Mrs. Hardy said. "It's in the middle of the block on Mortimer Street."

"Thanks, Mom," Joe said.

"But it's more than an hour until eleven o'clock," Fenton said. "What do you boys want to do before the club?"

Joe's stomach growled loudly. "Does that answer your question?" he asked.

"Who's in the mood for pancakes?" Frank asked.

"Me!" Joe said. "As long as they don't have blueberries. I hate blueberries in my pancakes."

After a late breakfast it was time to get to work. Frank and Joe were dropped off in front of Sammy's house, where they walked straight to the front door.

"Remember," Joe whispered as he rang the doorbell. "We're nutty for Nutty."

Sammy himself opened the door, still wearing his furry squirrel hat.

"We'd like to join your club," Joe declared.

Sammy raised a suspicious brow. "I thought you were Green Crawler fans," he said.

"Not anymore," Frank said.

"The Green Crawler balloon popped," Joe added. "What superhero has a wimpy balloon?"

"We want Nutty back in the parade too," Frank said. "That's why we're here."

Sammy seemed to think about it. He then stepped aside and said, "Okay. Come on in."

"All riiiiight!" Joe said. He snuck Frank a thumbs-up as they followed Sammy up the stairs. They were in!

Upstairs in Sammy's room Frank and Joe were not surprised to see several Nutty posters and bobbleheads, along with the other Nutty club members.

"Frank and Joe have finally wised up," Sammy announced to the group. "They're Nutty fans now."

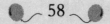

The other club members, some wearing squirrel hats, cheered their approval.

"Now that we're in the club," Frank said casually, "what did you guys do today?"

"Not so fast," Sammy said. "You can't join until you pass a test."

"Test?" Joe cried. "But it's Saturday!"

"We'll take it," Frank said quickly. "What do we have to do?"

A third grader Joe recognized as Cara Lund stepped forward.

"Just like Nutty, you have to stuff your mouth," Cara explained, "while answering questions about the show."

"With nuts?" Frank asked.

"Marshmallows," Cara said. "I'll ask Mrs. Kernkraut for a bowl."

After Cara left the room, Frank said, "Joe will go first. He's got a big mouth."

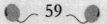

"Thanks." Joe smirked.

"Okay, Joe," Sammy said, tossing him a gray squirrel hat. "Sit in that chair and get ready."

"Sure," Joe said. He turned to Frank and whispered, "Look around for clues while I take the test."

"On it," Frank whispered back.

Joe put on the hat. He sat in the chair, rubbed his hands, and said, "I love marshmallows. Bring 'em on!"

Cara stepped into the room, carrying a bowl. "Your mom was out of marshmallows, Sammy," she said. "But she had plenty of fresh mushrooms."

Mushrooms? The only thing Joe hated more than blueberries was mushrooms.

Joe gagged several times. He clapped his hand over his mouth to try to keep from hurling.

"What's with him?" Sammy demanded.

"Joe's being funny!" Frank said quickly. He

60

couldn't let Joe eat all those mushrooms. He had to think of something—fast!

Frank made sure there was no TV in the room before saying, "There's a Nutty the Squirrel special on TV today."

"Seriously?" Cara gasped.

"It's in 3-D, but you don't need glasses," Frank said. He pointed to a Nutty clock on the wall. "And it's on now!"

"What are we waiting for?" Sammy asked the others. "Downstairs to the den!"

In a flash the club was out the door. Joe slumped forward and said, "Thanks, Frank."

"Sure," Frank said. "Now let's look for clues before they realize there is no show on TV."

The first place they looked was Sammy's desk.

"There!" Frank said. He pointed to the computer screen. The desktop picture showed the club and someone dressed as Nutty the Squirrel.

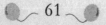

A banner above them read MEET NUTTY THE SQUIRREL with the date.

"That's today's date," Joe pointed out.

"It looks like they were at the arcade," Frank said. "So that's what the club did this morning. They met Nutty the Squirrel!"

Suddenly—

"There they are!" a voice shouted.

Frank and Joe turned to see Sammy and the rest of the club at the door. Alongside Sammy was his little sister, Sadie. Her eyes narrowed as she pointed at Frank and Joe.

"There they are!" Sadie shouted again. "The *spies*!"

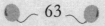

7

Zoom and Gloom

Great," Joe groaned under his breath. Maybe he should have given Sadie his Green Crawler claw.

"They were in the park," Sadie went on. "They were asking me silly questions about the club!"

"We should have remembered they were detectives," Sammy told the club.

"What do you want from us?" another member asked.

"We just want to find out who ripped the Green Crawler balloon," Frank said.

"What makes you think we ripped the balloon?" Sammy demanded.

"You didn't want the Green Crawler balloon in the parade," Joe explained. "And we saw you guys in the park this morning."

"We were walking through the park to get to the arcade," Sammy explained. "That's where Nutty was today!"

"The arcade is only three blocks from this house," Frank pointed out. "Why did you take the long way through the park?"

"We wanted to see if the parade was using the Nutty balloon after all," Cara said. "Too bad they weren't."

Joe took the hat off as he huddled with Frank. He whispered, "We saw the club go over to the balloon. They just looked at it and kept on walking."

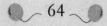

"Unless they came back," Frank replied.

Joe shook his head. "There's a clock in the picture," he said. "It was eight o'clock when they posed with Nutty."

"We saw the club at about seven forty-five," Frank said, doing the math. "They would need about fifteen minutes to walk from the park to the arcade—"

"Quit whispering about us," Sammy cut in. "And there was no Nutty cartoon on, either. You tricked us!"

"What do you expect from spies?" Sadie said, crossing her arms.

"The parade people were blaming Frank and me for ripping the balloon," Joe said. "We had to do something!"

"We know you didn't rip the balloon," Frank told the club. "Sorry."

The club members traded understanding looks.

"It's okay," Sammy said with a shrug. "You were just trying to find the person who really ripped the balloon."

"You can still join the club, if you'd like," Cara said. She picked up the bowl and smiled. "We've got plenty of mushrooms!"

Joe clapped his hand over his mouth. "Frank," he murmured through his fingers. "We've got to get out of here."

Quickly Frank thanked the club, then excused

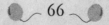

himself and Joe. The brothers raced past Sammy, Sadie, and the rest of the club.

"You're greener than the Crawler!" Frank said when they were outside. "Do you want to go home?"

Joe took a deep breath of fresh air. He shook his head. "I'm okay," he said. "Just don't mention . . . you know what."

"Hey, Frank, Joe!" someone called.

The brothers turned to see their friend Phil Cohen. Phil had a knack for inventing all kinds of gadgets. This time he was holding a long rod. At one end was a wheel-shaped handle. At the other end was a metal box with green and red lights.

"What's that?" Joe asked.

"My latest invention," Phil said as he came closer. "The King of Ka-Ching Coin and Metal Detector!"

"A metal detector?" Joe repeated.

"It's for finding stuff that people dropped," Phil explained. "Like jewelry, money—maybe buried treasure."

"I've seen metal detectors before, Phil," Frank said. "What makes this one so special?"

"I made it myself!" Phil declared proudly.

Frank and Joe watched as Phil waved the device over the sidewalk. It began to beep. Phil smiled as he picked up a quarter.

"See?" Phil said. "It's already paying off!"

Frank and Joe watched as Phil continued up the street.

"What will Phil think of next?" Frank said.

"Hopefully, a Who Ripped the Balloon gadget," Joe joked. "We could use one of those right now!"

Suddenly—*ROOOOOOOOOOAARRRRRRRRR!*

What was that? The brothers spun around and gasped. Zooming up the middle of the sidewalk was a red motorbike.

Frank grabbed his brother's arm. The motorbike was speeding straight toward them!

"Joe!" Frank shouted. "Look out!"

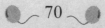

8

Musical Scares

Frank and Joe jumped back in the nick of time. They watched the red motorbike zoom by. The driver wore a black helmet and jacket.

"Jeez, Frank!" Joe cried as the bike careened around the corner. "Who just tried to run us over?"

"I don't know," Frank said. "I couldn't see the driver's face under the helmet."

"Didn't we see a red motorbike in the park earlier this morning?" Joe asked. "Maybe it belonged to someone working on the parade."

"Why would someone in the parade want to run us over?" Frank asked.

"Let's figure that out somewhere else," Joe said, glancing over his shoulder, "in case that crazy driver decides to come back."

The brothers hurried home and straight to their tree house. Joe sat in his favorite beanbag chair, while Frank stood by the dry-erase board.

"Why?" Frank said, writing the word on the board. "Why would anyone from the parade want to run us over?"

"Maybe it was a warning," Joe said. "The driver might have heard us tell Kevin we'd look for the balloon ripper."

"Or maybe they *read* about it!" Frank said.

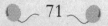

"Read about it?" Joe repeated. "What do you mean?"

"We forgot to erase the six *W*s we wrote on the basketball court," Frank said. "They had the suspects' names and everything!"

"How would they know it was us?" Joe asked.

"There aren't many 'detectives' in town— maybe they heard us when we told Lynn and Kevin we would find the real suspect," Frank said.

The brothers had only one suspect left. Frank wrote the name Kit on the board in big letters.

"Let's look for Kit now," Joe said.

Frank shook his head. "I think we should take a break," he said. "We'll look for Kit tomorrow."

"But the parade is tomorrow!" Joe exclaimed.

"It doesn't start until two o'clock," Frank said. "That gives us time to question Kit—if we can find her."

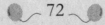

Joe remembered the laptop they'd brought up to the tree house. He grabbed it and began a search.

"What are you looking for?" Frank asked.

"Maybe the Bayport Boomerangs posted their practice schedule," Joe said. "I still can't believe we get Wi-Fi up here!"

Joe found Bayport High School's website. He clicked on "Bayport Boomerangs" and found their schedule.

"The Boomerangs have a pre-parade practice tomorrow at eight o'clock!" Joe pointed out.

"Kit will be there too," Frank figured. "We've got to go to the school tomorrow, Joe."

"Okay," Joe said. "But let's get someone to drive us there."

"How come?" Frank asked.

"In case Kit brings her motorbike," Joe replied, and frowned.

Frank and Joe were driven to the high school Sunday morning by their aunt Gertrude.

Aunt Gertrude lived in the apartment above the Hardys' garage. She was an early riser, even on Sundays.

"Thanks again for driving us, Aunt Gertrude," Frank said.

"No problem!" Aunt Gertrude said as she drove up to the school. "Bayport High is on the

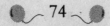

way to my bird-watchers' club in the park. If we're lucky, we'll spot a red-tailed hawk today!"

Joe leaned over to Frank and whispered, "And if we're lucky, we'll spot Kit!"

Frank and Joe waved good-bye to Aunt Gertrude as she drove off. As the brothers walked toward the school, they checked out the parking lot. No red motorbikes.

"Unless Kit parks it behind the school," Frank decided. Then—

"There she is!" Joe said. He pointed to the football field. The Bayport Boomerangs were marching back and forth. Running alongside them in her band uniform was Kit.

"Kit won't talk to us while they're practicing," Frank decided. "We'll have to wait until they're finished."

"Can we wait inside the school?" Joe asked. "I want to see if there's a snack machine."

"Snack?" Frank cried. "Didn't we just have breakfast?"

"That was a whole hour ago, Frank!" Joe said.

Frank and Joe entered the school through the main door. They headed up a long hallway, looking for a snack machine.

Glass cases filled with trophies lined one wall. Classrooms took up the other wall. One door was open. Joe peeked inside. He saw a piano, a drum set, and a board covered with musical notes.

"This must be the music room," Joe pointed out.

Frank read the teacher's name on the door.

"This is Kit's classroom," Frank declared. "Let's go inside and look for clues."

The brothers slipped into the room. Kit's desk stood in front of the board. The desk and chair were covered with loose papers and sheet music.

"This is messier than my room!" Joe declared.

"Don't touch anything," Frank whispered. "Just look!"

But as Frank and Joe neared the desk, they heard a voice out in the hall. The brothers froze in their tracks.

"That's Kit!" Joe hissed.

"She can't find us snooping in here," Frank whispered. "We have to hide!"

9

Buried Treasure

There!" Joe said, pointing to the drums.

Frank and Joe ducked behind the drum set. They held their breath as Kit entered the classroom.

"That's right, Sal," Kit was saying. "I didn't think we could do it, but we did."

Frank and Joe peeked over the drums. Kit was at her desk, talking on her cell phone.

"We took care of the Green Crawler," Kit

said, chuckling. "Now let's see who the star of the parade will be!"

Joe's mouth dropped open. He turned to Frank and whispered, "Did you hear that?" He pointed back at Kit. "Kit just confessed. She—"

CRASH!

Joe's arm knocked a cymbal off the drum set and onto the

floor. The brothers cringed as it rattled loudly across the tile.

Frank and Joe crouched, as still as statues—until Kit shouted, "Who's there?"

The brothers peeked out again. Kit was coming toward the drum set.

"Hey," Kit said, narrowing her eyes. "Aren't you the kids who were kicked out of the parade yesterday?"

"That was us," Frank admitted, standing up.

"Well, what do you want in my classroom?" Kit demanded.

"Um . . . music lessons?" Joe squeaked.

Kit folded her arms and said, "Try again."

"Joe and I wanted to find out who ripped the Green Crawler balloon yesterday," Frank said as they walked out from behind the drums.

"You just said on your phone that you took care

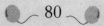

of the Green Crawler," Joe said bravely. "So it must have been you."

Kit stared at the boys, then began to laugh.

"I didn't rip the Green Crawler balloon!" Kit said. "I meant that my band finally learned the Green Crawler tune!"

"You mean the song Kevin wanted you to play?" Frank asked.

Kit nodded and said, "I didn't think they'd learn it so fast—but the Boomerangs are the best!"

"Okay," Joe said slowly. "Then what were you doing, crawling under the balloon yesterday?"

"I was looking for my lost watch," Kit said.

"Why under the balloon?" Frank asked.

"Because we had been practicing on the field before they laid out the balloon," Kit explained. "I was pretty sure I dropped it there."

Joe nodded at the conductor's baton sticking

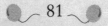

out of Kit's pocket. "You still could have poked a hole in the balloon with that thing," he said.

"I didn't have my baton with me then, smart guy," Kit said. "I didn't find my watch, either."

Joe shot Frank a glance. Was Kit telling the truth?

"I don't need a watch to know I'm wasting time here," Kit said. "Why don't you kids leave so I can get back to work?"

The brothers walked toward the door. Joe noticed Frank staring at a nearby coatrack. Hanging on it was a tan coat and brown scarf.

Once in the hall Frank said, "I didn't see any motorcycle helmet or jacket."

"She could have come here in a car," Joe said. He shook his head. "I just don't know if I believe Kit about that lost watch."

"Or about her not having the baton," Frank added. "I just wish we had some kind of proof."

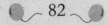 82

A cold blast of fall air greeted the brothers as they walked outside. Frank dug his hands into his jacket pockets for his gloves. Instead, he felt his camera—still there from the day before.

Frank pulled out his camera and checked the last few shots.

"What are you looking for?" Joe asked.

"Here's a shot I took of the Bayport Boomerangs practicing," Frank pointed out. "Right before we saw Kit under the balloon."

Frank enlarged the picture. Instead of Kit, a student was waving a conductor's baton.

"That's the same pointy baton!" Joe observed.

"So Kit *didn't* have her baton under the balloon," Frank said.

"But how do we know she was really looking for her watch?" Joe asked.

"Hey!" Frank said, his eyes lighting up. "We can borrow Phil's metal detector and look for the watch."

"And if we find it," Joe said, "we'll know she was telling the truth!"

Aunt Gertrude was thrilled with her successful birdwatching from that morning. She offered to drive the boys anywhere they wanted, and the boys figured they should take advantage of her good mood.

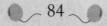

"To Phil Cohen's house, Aunt Gertrude," Joe said. He quickly added, "Please."

From Phil's house the brothers walked straight to the park—with the King of Ka-Ching Coin and Metal Detector.

"What if we find something gross with this thing?" Joe asked. "Like somebody's retainer."

Suddenly—*BEEP, BEEP, BEEP!*

"We found something!" Frank exclaimed.

Frank and Joe looked down to see a metal button, half covered with dirt.

"It's not a watch," Joe sighed. "But at least we know this thing works."

The detector went off again. This time it found a dime. A few feet away it beeped over a metal key chain with no keys.

Joe was getting impatient. It was a big field. What if they never found a watch? But then—

BEEP, BEEP, BEEP!

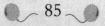

Something silver was sticking up out of the dirt. Frank pulled it out and said, "It's a watch!"

"How do we know it's Kit's watch?" Joe asked.

Frank flipped it over. On the back was an engraving that read *To Kit for 10 years of band excellence.*

"Kit told the truth about losing her watch here," Joe said. "But now we have no more suspects."

"I know," Frank sighed. "We'd better keep this and return it to Kit."

He was about to slip the watch into his pocket when—

BEEP, BEEEEEEP!

The brothers looked down at something shiny.

"It looks like a pocketknife," Frank said.

Carefully Joe picked it up. It *was* a pocket-knife—with green fibers stuck to the blade!

"Green like the Green Crawler," Frank said. "The balloon could have been cut with this knife, but whose is it?"

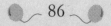

"Let's ask Dad to run a fingerprint test on it!" Joe said.

"Not enough time," Frank said. "The parade starts in less than two hours."

"But what if the balloon ripper tries again?" Joe asked. "At the parade?"

"Don't even think of going to that parade," Frank said. "If Kevin or Lynn sees us, they'll send us straight home."

"Unless . . . no one sees us," Joe said with a slow smile. "Frank, I have an idea!"

10

Raid on Parade

It was Sunday afternoon, and it was time for Frank and Joe to go undercover again. Covering their heads and faces were rubber Green Crawler masks.

"Hey, Frank?" Joe asked, his voice muffled under the rubber. "Do you think we look like balloon handlers?"

"The most important thing is that we don't look like ourselves," Frank replied. "We're lucky the party shop had leftover masks from Halloween."

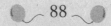

"We'll be luckier if we find the real balloon rip-per," Joe said.

The brothers reached Bay Street. A crowd stood in front of Snyder's Department Store, waiting for the parade to kick off.

"My nose itches!" Joe complained. "And I can't scratch it under this mask!"

"Tough it out," Frank whispered through his own mask. "We can't let anyone know it's us."

"Frank, Joe, over here!" Chet's voice called.

The brothers froze. They turned to see Chet waving from the crowd.

"How did you know it was us?" Frank asked.

"We're wearing masks," Joe added.

"You're also wearing the same sneakers you always wear," Chet said, pointing down at their feet.

"Oh," Joe said.

"Don't let anyone know we're here, Chet,"

Frank warned. "We're not supposed to be in the parade."

Chet wrinkled his nose with surprise.

"But Joe won the contest!" Chet said. "You're supposed to be balloon handlers!"

"We'll explain later," Frank said, looking around. "Where is the balloon, anyway?"

"It's around the corner," Chet said. "I got a peek of it, and it's awesome!"

They were joined by Iola, who was carrying two cups of hot chocolate. She looked down at the brothers' feet and said, "Hi, Frank. Hi, Joe."

Joe rolled his eyes behind his mask. "So much for undercover."

Frank and Joe walked past the crowd and turned the corner. As Chet had said, the block was lined with parade floats, clowns, and the Bayport Boomerangs. Behind the band was the Green Crawler balloon, weighted down by

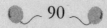

sandbags. Even on the ground, it towered over everything.

"It *is* awesome!" Frank exclaimed.

As they were approaching the balloon, Joe glanced down an alley. There was a red motorbike leaning against a wall.

"Frank, look!" Joe said.

The brothers slipped into the alley to examine the bike. It looked exactly like the bike that had almost run them over.

"So the driver *is* in the parade," Frank decided. "But who is it?"

Joe examined the helmet for a name. All he found was a decal above the visor. The decal looked like an insect.

"Maybe it's a grasshopper," Joe wondered.

Frank didn't look at the sticker. He tugged at Joe's arm and said, "Come on. We've got to get to that balloon!"

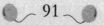

No one tried to stop Frank and Joe as they walked toward the Green Crawler balloon. The masks were doing the trick.

Joe gazed up at the balloon. "It's bigger than our house!" he exclaimed.

Standing around the balloon were the handlers. Most were not wearing their masks or handler gloves yet.

"There's Brett," Frank whispered.

Brett was standing off to the side. His eyes darted back and forth as he rubbed his chin thoughtfully.

"What's he looking for?" Joe whispered.

Suddenly Frank noticed something on Brett's hand. "Joe," he hissed. "Brett's tattoo —it's a praying mantis!"

"You said the guy who played Mo Mantis had a praying mantis tattoo," Joe said. "Could that guy have been Brett?"

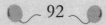

The brothers inched over to Brett. Joe checked out the tattoo and gasped.

"Frank!" Joe hissed. "That wasn't a grasshopper sticker I saw on the motorcycle helmet. It was a praying mantis!"

"So that was Brett's bike in the alley," Frank whispered. "And it was Brett who tried to run us over!"

"I don't get it," Joe whispered. "If Brett is Mo Mantis, why is he working as a balloon handler?"

Brett began walking slowly toward the balloon. Something was sticking out of his back pocket.

"Brett's got something in his back pocket. It looks like scissors!" Joe said. "Let's follow him."

Frank and Joe carefully followed Brett around the balloon. Brett stopped beside the Green Crawler's giant head. There were no other handlers nearby.

The brothers stood back, secretly watching

Brett. He pulled out his scissors and pointed them at the balloon. But before he could jab—

"Stop!" Joe yelled.

Frank and Joe pulled off their masks as they ran toward Brett. When Brett saw them, he scowled.

"What are you kids doing here?" Brett demanded. "I thought you were sacked."

"What's with the scissors?" Joe asked. "Can't find your pocketknife?"

"What about a pocketknife?" Brett demanded.

"We found one right where the balloon was, in the park," Frank replied. "It had green stuff on it."

"FYI," Joe added.

"Where is it?" Brett demanded angrily. "Give me back my knife!"

"Your knife, huh?" Joe asked. "Was that a confession?"

Brett growled under his breath as he took a step toward Frank and Joe. Before the brothers could call for help, they heard a voice shout, "Brett Marshall, stop right there. And drop those scissors!"

The brothers turned to see Lynn, Kevin, and Mitch Snyder of Snyder's Department Store. The three were dressed as toy soldiers for the parade.

"What's going on?" Lynn asked.

"We have to get that balloon off the ground in ten minutes!" Kevin exclaimed.

"The Green Crawler balloon will never get off the ground if Brett has his way," Frank said.

"Or should we say . . . Mo Mantis?" Joe said.

The three stared at Brett.

"Was that you playing Mo Mantis at the mall?" Mitch asked.

Brett's eyes lit up at the mention of Mo. "That was me under that mask!" he said proudly.

Joe turned to Kevin, Lynn, and Mitch. "We found Brett's pocketknife in the park," he said. "We think he ripped the Green Crawler balloon!"

"Brett?" Lynn said, folding her arms. "Do you have something to tell us?"

Brett's face turned redder and redder, until he finally said, "Yeah, I slashed that dumb balloon, and I'd do it again!"

"Why?" Kevin cried.

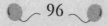

"Because the Mo Mantis balloon should be in the parade, not the Green Crawler," Brett explained. "The bigger a star Mo is, the bigger a star I am."

"Is that why you volunteered as a handler?" Lynn asked. "So you could get at the balloon?"

Brett nodded. "I ripped the balloon while we were spreading it out on the grass," he said. "I hadn't planned on losing my pocketknife."

"Did you plan on running us over with your motorbike?" Frank asked angrily.

"You were in my way!" Brett growled.

Joe saw Lynn motion to two guys wearing shades. They were Dash and Boris, Taylor Smyth's bodyguards.

"Tell the cops about it, balloon boy," Dash said as he grabbed Brett's arm.

"Let's go," Boris said, grabbing his other arm, "so these nice people can have a parade."

Clowns, balloon handlers, dancers, and the Bayport Boomerangs stepped back as the bodyguards led Brett away.

"Mo Mantis rules!" Brett shouted. "The Green Crawler drools!"

Joe looked up at Kevin. "Does this mean there'll be no more Mo Mantis in the movies?" he asked.

"Don't worry, Joe," Lynn said, and chuckled. "They'll just get another guy to play the villain."

"How about Adam Ackerman?" Frank joked.

"Okay, everybody!" Lynn called to the handlers. "Let's get the Green Crawler off the ground!"

While handlers untied the Green Crawler balloon, Kevin thanked Frank and Joe for their help.

"No problem." Joe smiled. "You can tell Kit we found her watch, too."

The brothers were turning to leave when Kevin called, "Wait! Aren't you guys going to join the other handlers?"

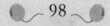

"You mean in the parade?" Frank asked, surprised.

"Sure!" Kevin said. "The Green Crawler may save the world from Mo Mantis, but you saved the parade."

"Does that make us superheroes too?" Joe asked.

"I don't know about that," Kevin said, smiling. "But you two are *super* detectives."

Frank's and Joe's balloon handler gloves thumped as they high-fived. They were back in the Fall Fest parade. And the minute they got back to their tree house, they would write on the board in huge letters . . .

SECRET FILES CASE #13: SOLVED!

Did you **LOVE** this book?

Want to get access to great books for **FREE?**

Join

Simon & Schuster
IN THE **bookloop**

where you can

★ Read great books for FREE! ★

Get exclusive excerpts

Chat with your friends

Log on to join now!

everloop.com/loops/in-the-book

CAN'T GET ENOUGH OF THE

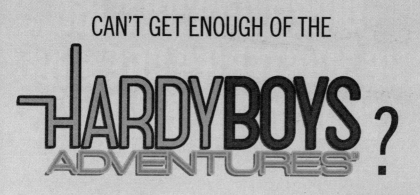

HARDYBOYS ADVENTURES?

Stay connected to Frank and Joe online!

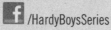

HardyBoysSeries.com

/HardyBoysSeries

ALADDIN

WHEN YOU'RE A KID,
the MYSTERIES ARE JUST
that MUCH *BIGGER*...

NANCY DREW
AND THE CLUE CREW
SECRET SAND SLEUTHS

All-new comics from
PAPERCUTZ!

© 2012 SIMON & SCHUSTER CHILDREN'S PUBLISHING. ALL RIGHTS RESERVED.

New mystery.
New suspense.
New danger.

All-new
Nancy Drew
series!

BY CAROLYN KEENE

EBOOK EDITIONS ALSO AVAILABLE
From Aladdin | KIDS.SimonandSchuster.com

Join Zeus and his friends as they set off on the adventure of a lifetime.

31901055230967

EBOOK EDITIONS ALSO AVAILABLE
From Aladdin • KIDS.SimonandSchuster.com